D0897366

THE TALE OF DESPEREAUX

by
Kate DiCamillo

Teacher Guide

Written by
Nomi Waldman

Note

The Candlewick Press hardback edition of the book, ©2003 by Kate DiCamillo, was used to prepare this guide. Page references may differ in other editions. Novel ISBN: 0-7636-1722-9

Please note: Please assess the appropriateness of this book for the age level and maturity of your students prior to reading and discussing it with them.

ISBN 1-58130-523-0

Copyright infringement is a violation of Federal Law.

To order, contact your local school supply store, or—

Novel Units, Inc.
P.O. Box 97
Bulverde, TX 78163-0097

Web site: www.educyberstor.com

Lori Mammen, Editorial Director
Andrea M. Harris, Production Manager/Production Specialist
Kim Kraft, Product Development Manager/Curriculum Specialist
Suzanne K. Mammen, Curriculum Specialist
Heather Johnson, Product Development Specialist
Jill Reed, Product Development Specialist
Nancy Smith, Product Development Specialist
Pramilla Freitas, Production Specialist
Adrienne Speer, Production Specialist

Table of Contents

Skills and Strategies

Comprehension
Identifying attributes, compare/contrast, creative and critical thinking, predicting, evaluating, supporting judgments, noting important details

Writing
Glossary, poetry, journal, riddle

Listening/Speaking
Discussion, role-playing, dramatic reading, interview, TV/film

Vocabulary
Synonym, antonym, context clues, definition, target words

Literary Elements
Metaphor, simile, story map, plot, setting, theme, character analysis

Across the Curriculum
Social Studies—research, recipes; Science—research; Art—illustration, puppets

Genre: fantasy

Setting: a castle in an imaginary kingdom

Point of View: third person

Themes: impossible love, light vs. dark, determination, loyalty

Conflict: person/animal vs. society, person vs. animal, person vs. person, animal vs. animal

Style: narrative

Tone: initially bright, but darkening as events unfold

Date of First Publication: 2003

Summary

Despereaux Tilling is a castle mouse and unlike any other mouse. First, there is his unusually small physique and large ears. Then there is his desire to read books rather than nibble on their pages. In this way, he becomes inspired by a story of courtly love and becomes enamored of the Princess Pea. To his joy, she also takes notice of him. However, this very unmouselike behavior puts Despereaux's life in danger. The other mice banish him to the castle dungeon, where fierce rats lurk, eager to devour Despereaux. Among them is Chiaroscuro—Roscuro for short—a rat with an uncharacteristic love of light. This attraction leads him to explore the upper levels of the castle, including the banquet hall. His accidental landing in the queen's soup, though, is too much for her, and she dies of shock. Into this situation comes Miggery Sow, a kitchen helper whose life of mistreatment has left her nearly deaf but not without a dream—to take Pea's place as princess. Roscuro, believing himself slighted by Princess Pea, takes advantage of Mig's fantasy to get revenge on the princess. With Mig's help, he leads Pea deep into the dungeon. Despereaux, meanwhile, has escaped his expected fate because of a friendly jailer eager to hear the stories that he recalls from his reading. Despereaux is determined to do what any faithful knight would do for his lady—rescue her from danger.

About the Author

For much of her life, Kate DiCamillo lived in the South. After graduating from the University of Florida, she took various jobs, including working at Circus World and Disney World. She began telling people that she was a writer even before she actually wrote anything. When DiCamillo moved to Minnesota, a chilly winter kept her indoors, and she began to write. Her first novel, the best-selling *Because of Winn-Dixie* (2000), was a Newbery Honor book. Her second novel, *The Tiger Rising* (2001), was a National Book Award Finalist. *The Tale of Despereaux* won the 2004 Newbery Medal. DiCamillo says she wrote this book because a friend's son asked for a book with an unlikely hero with large ears.

Additional Information

The Tale of Despereaux, though modern, has echoes of many traditional tales. One familiar device is the author's tendency to address the audience directly as "dear reader." Another is the medieval convention of courtly love, which involved the love of a knight for a lady, usually one of high station. The key to the relationship was the understanding that the lady's love was probably unattainable. This fantasy novel is also in the tradition of European fairy tales, with many dark elements. Though there are no fairies or magical creatures, as in traditional fairy tales, the story does involve creatures and events that could not exist in real life, such as a mouse that can speak and read. There is also the conventional battle of good vs. evil. DiCamillo's modern twist, though, is that some of the main characters fall into a gray area, having both good and bad qualities. One example of this is in the character Chiaroscuro, whose name means a mixture of light and dark, e.g., good and bad qualities. Similarly, the ending, while satisfying to the reader, leaves the characters with less than complete success and happiness.

Main Characters

Despereaux Tilling—a mouse born in King Phillip's castle; loves to read stories; banished to the castle dungeon for falling in love with the princess

Princess Pea—a beautiful girl who is kind to all living things

Chiaroscuro (Roscuro)—a rat in the castle dungeon; unusual in that he loves light

Miggery Sow (Mig)—a slow-witted serving girl in the castle; mistreated by Uncle; wishes to be a princess

Secondary Characters

Lester and Antoinette Tilling—Despereaux's parents

Furlough—Despereaux's brother

Merlot—Despereaux's sister

King Phillip—Princess Pea's father

Queen Rosemary—Princess Pea's mother

Gregory—the jailer in the castle dungeon; enjoys Despereaux's stories

Botticelli Remorso—an evil rat living in the castle dungeon

Uncle—cruel man responsible for Miggery Sow's care; causes her loss of hearing because he hits her on the head

Hovis—the castle threadmaster

Louise—a member of the castle serving staff

Cook—a member of the castle serving staff

Initiating Activities

Use one or more of the following to introduce the novel.

1. Previewing the Book: Ask students to make predictions about the book based on their examination of the following: title page, dedication, table of contents page, author's invitation to the reader.

2. Prior Knowledge: Invite students to share what they know about kings, princesses, castles, and dungeons from other stories they have read. Suggest that they use what they know to make predictions about this book.

3. Art: Ask students to locate the name of the illustrator of *The Tale of Despereaux*. Have them sample several of his illustrations, e.g., the front and back covers, pp. 14, 31, 80, and discuss the mood that each conveys. Then have each student create an illustration of his/her own to express a chosen mood.

4. Brainstorming: Divide the class into three groups. Assign each group one of the following words: rodent, princess, dungeon. Have students complete an Attribute Web (see page 6 of this guide) for their word. Display the completed webs in the classroom.

5. Plot Development: Have students work in pairs or small groups to complete the graphic on page 7 of this guide.

Vocabulary Activities

1. Rhymes and Chimes: Have each student choose one vocabulary word from each section and write a riddle, rhyme, poem, or song that describes that word. Students should trade descriptions and determine which vocabulary word is being described.

2. Synonym/Antonym Match: Divide the class into six groups and assign each group a section's vocabulary list. Have each group write a synonym and an antonym for each word on a small piece of paper. Then students should exchange papers with another group and match each synonym/antonym pair to the appropriate vocabulary word.

3. Word Maps: Have students complete Word Maps (see page 8 of this guide) for selected vocabulary words from *The Tale of Despereaux*.

4. Target Words: Have students draw pictures of three to four vocabulary words and have classmates guess the target words. Some suggested words for *The Tale of Despereaux* are: siblings (20), burly (63), abyss (69), and tapestries (103).

5. Glossary: Invite students to create their own glossary of challenging or unfamiliar words as they read the book.

Attribute Web

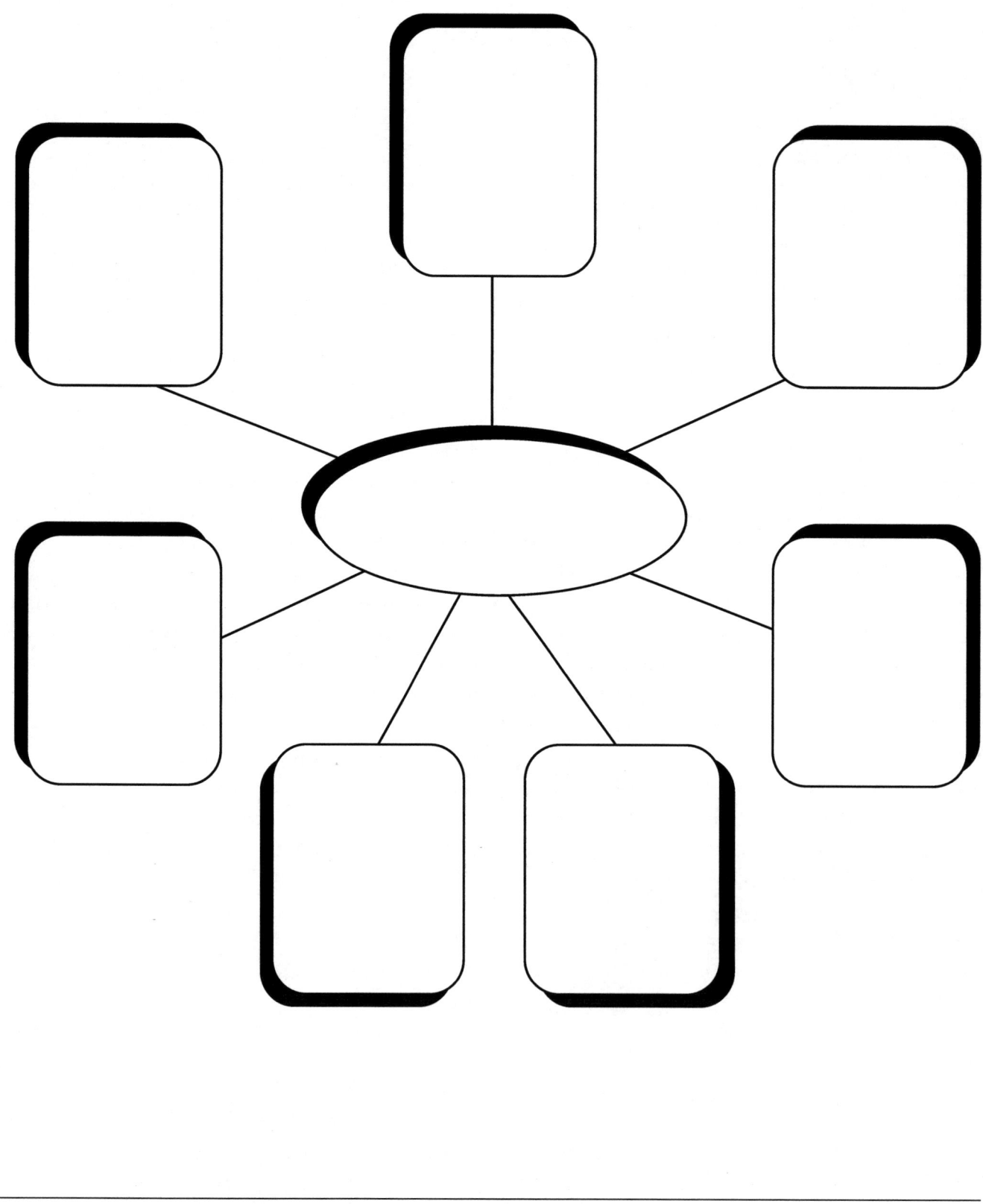

Be a Detective!

Directions: Check out the book by looking at the cover and thumbing through the pages. Then, ask yourself who, what, where, when, why, and how. Write your questions in the spaces below. Exchange papers with another group and answer the questions.

Who?

_____
_____
_____
_____

What?

_____
_____
_____
_____

Where?

_____
_____
_____

When?

_____
_____
_____
_____

Why?

_____
_____
_____
_____
_____

How?

_____
_____
_____
_____
_____

Word Map

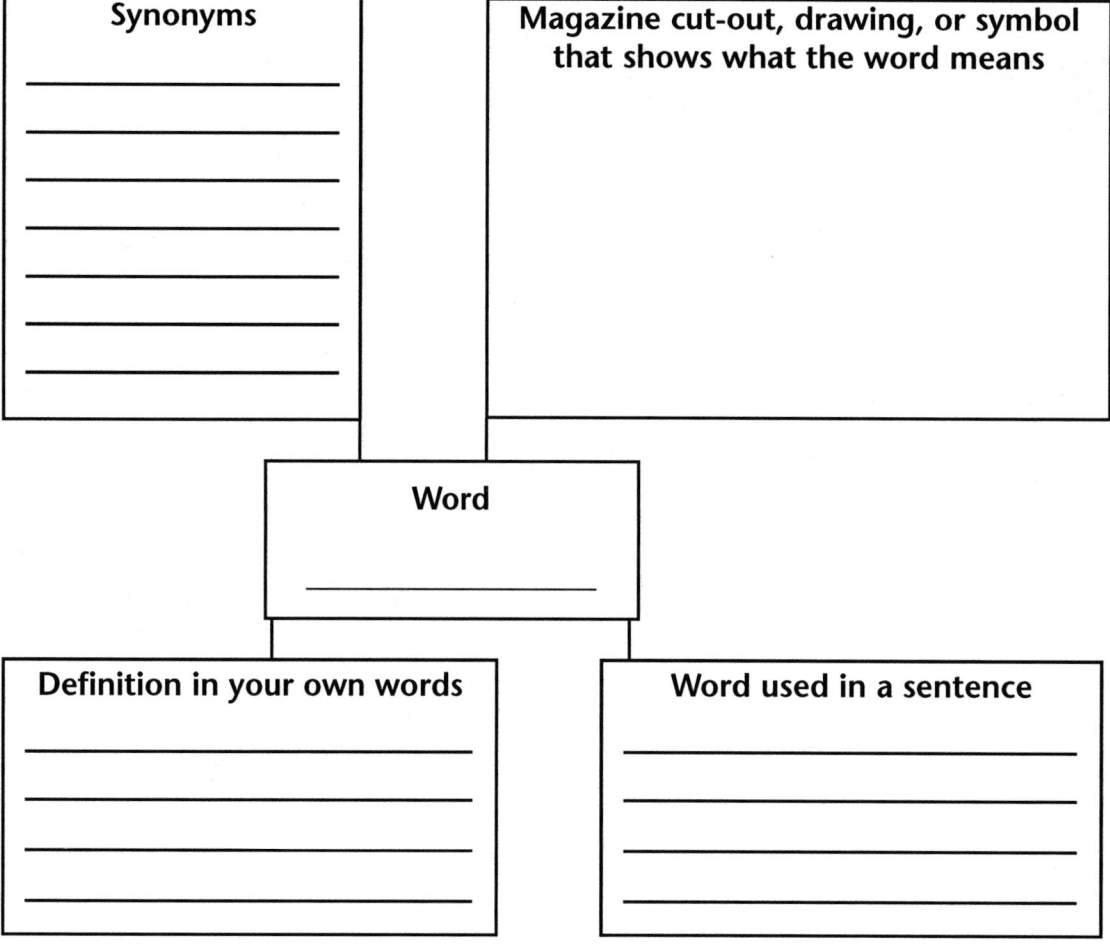

Synonyms

_____
_____
_____
_____
_____
_____

Magazine cut-out, drawing, or symbol that shows what the word means

Word

_____

Definition in your own words

_____
_____
_____
_____

Word used in a sentence

_____
_____
_____
_____

Character Attribute Web

Directions: The attribute web below will help you gather clues the author provides about a character in the novel. Fill in the blanks with words and phrases that tell how the character acts and looks, as well as what the character says and feels.

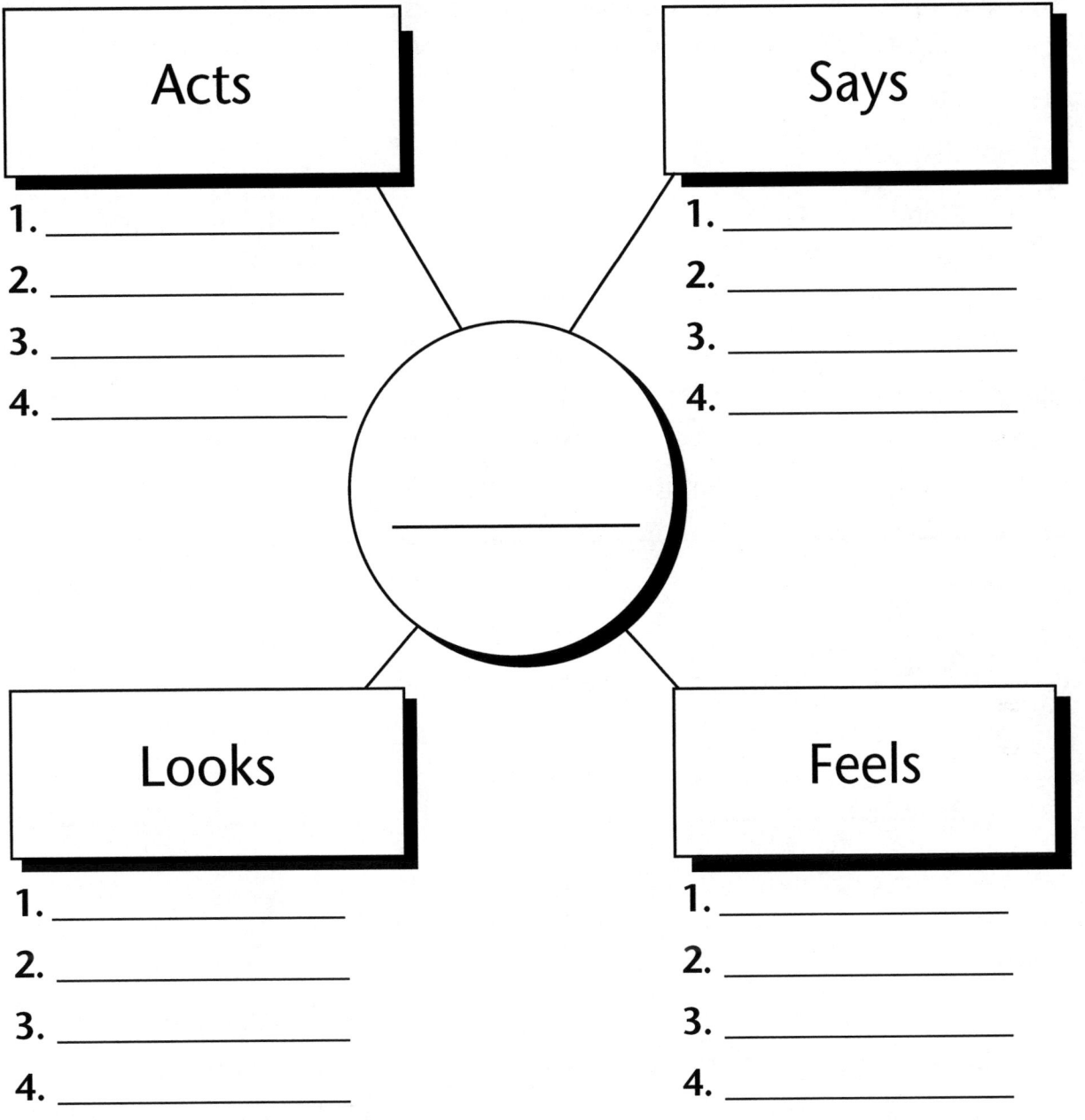

Acts
1. _____
2. _____
3. _____
4. _____

Says
1. _____
2. _____
3. _____
4. _____

Looks
1. _____
2. _____
3. _____
4. _____

Feels
1. _____
2. _____
3. _____
4. _____

Metaphors and Similes

A **metaphor** is a comparison between two unlike objects. For example, "he was a human tree." A **simile** is a comparison between two unlike objects that uses the words *like* or *as*. For example, "the color of her eyes was like the cloudless sky."

Directions: Complete the chart below by listing metaphors and similes from the novel, as well as the page numbers on which they are found. Identify metaphors with an "M" and similes with an "S." Translate the comparisons in your own words, and then list the objects being compared.

Metaphors/Similes	Ideas/Objects Being Compared
1. Translation:	
2. Translation:	
3. Translation:	

Effects of Reading

Directions: When reading, each part of a book may affect you in a different way. Think about how parts of the novel affected you in different ways. Did some parts make you laugh? cry? want to do something to help someone? Below, list one part of the book that touched each of the following parts of the body: your head (made you think), your heart (made you feel), your funny bone (made you laugh), or your feet (spurred you to action).

Your head

Your heart

Your funny bone

Your feet

Story Map

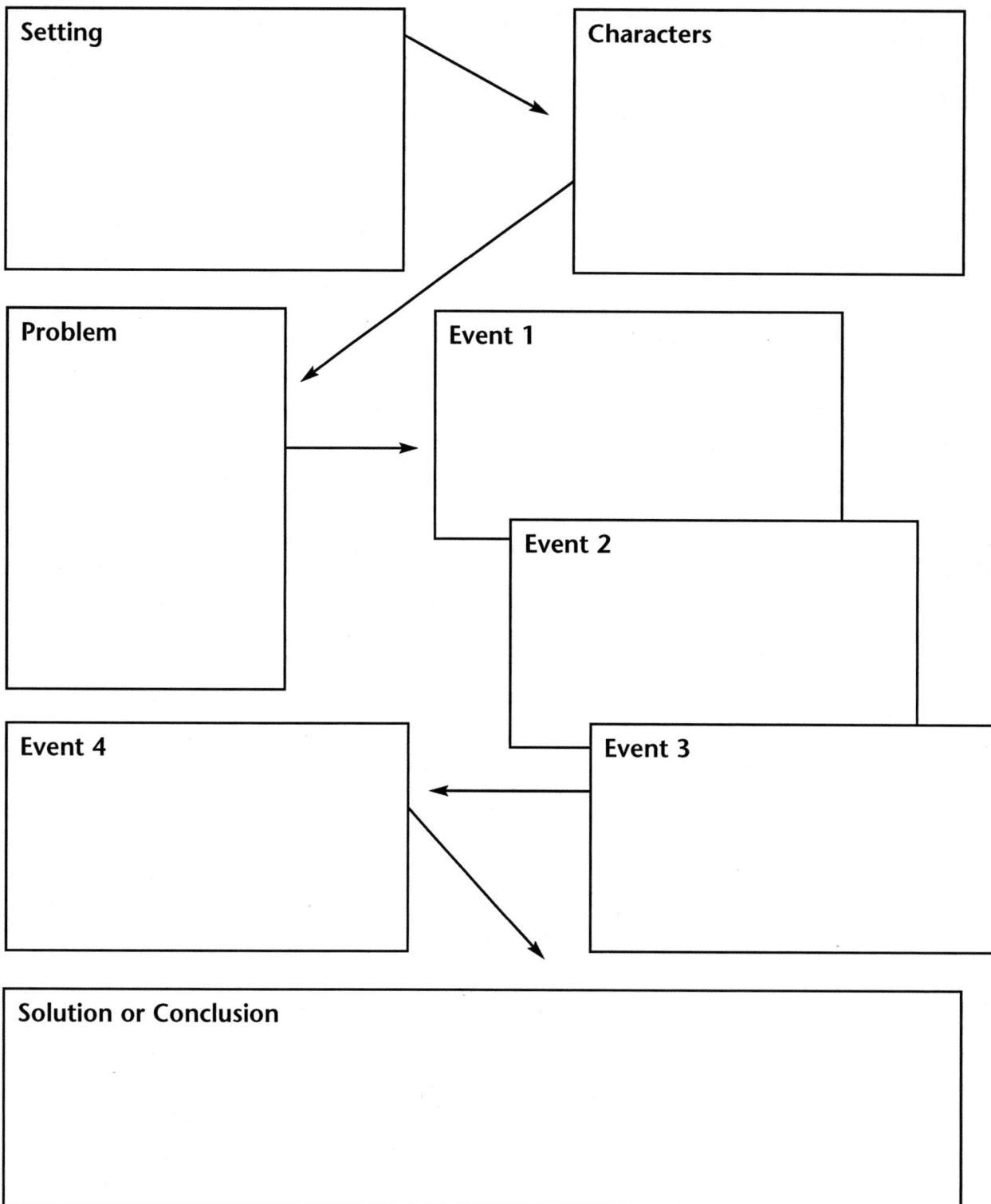

Setting

Characters

Problem

Event 1

Event 2

Event 3

Event 4

Solution or Conclusion

Book the First, Chapters 1–7, pp. 11–41

Despereaux Tilling is a castle mouse that is very unlike other mice. His siblings try to "educate him in the ways of being a mouse," but Despereaux enjoys being different. When he reads a story of courtly love, Despereaux quickly falls in love with Princess Pea. To his surprise and joy, she also takes notice of him. Even though he knows that a mouse should never allow a human to see him, Despereaux can't help but speak to the princess. However, his brother Furlough sees him and tells their father.

Vocabulary
disappointment (12)
tragedy (12)
intent (18)
siblings (20)
molding (21)
indignant (24)
circumstances (27)
incredible (30)
adoringly (32)
protested (38)
ancient (39)

Discussion Questions

1. What unusual circumstances surround Despereaux's birth? Discuss how those events affect the way the other mice think of Despereaux. *(He is very small with large ears. Strangest of all is the fact that his eyes are wide open, and he can see. The family immediately decides that there is something wrong with him, and therefore he is a disappointment to his parents. Later, whenever he does something that is not typical of a normal mouse, other mice refer to the strangeness of his birth or remind him that he is a disappointment. pp. 11–25)*

2. What does the author mean when she says, "Reader, you must know that an interesting fate (sometimes involving rats, sometimes not) awaits almost everyone, mouse or man, who does not conform" (p. 25)? *(She is suggesting that it is not just mice but people, too, who need to be aware that not conforming [that is, not doing things the way they are usually done] may cause problems that require courage to overcome.)*

3. What can Despereaux do to convince the other mice that he is not so different from them? Do you think he should do so? Why or why not? *(He can do exactly as his siblings and the other mice do with no variation, especially as they have already made up their minds that he is odd. Answers will vary.)*

4. What "thankless task" do Despereaux's siblings abandon and why? What would you have done in their place? *(They stop trying to educate him in the ways of being a mouse. They feel as though it is a hopeless waste of time because Despereaux is too strange. Answers will vary. pp. 20–26)*

5. What fear motivates Lester to call the Mouse Council in order to discuss his son's behavior? *(He fears that Despereaux's contact with humans might endanger the entire mouse community, that is, that "mice must act like mice or else there is bound to be trouble" p. 35.)*

6. On page 41 of the novel, the author writes, "He was, alas, a mouse deeply in love." Knowing that the word alas means "sadly" or "unfortunately," predict what you think Despereaux's future will be like. *(The use of alas should, along with other clues, suggest that Despereaux will have problems in the near future.)*

Supplementary Activities

1. Character Analysis: Based on what you have learned about them so far, compare King Phillip's character and that of his daughter, Princess Pea. Begin by listing the qualities that you admire in each person. Put a plus sign in front of those items. Then list those characteristics you do not think are admirable, putting a minus sign before those. Which person received more plus signs?

2. Literary Devices: Identify the following quotations as using simile, metaphor, or personification, then briefly explain what effect the author is trying to achieve.
   a. "The April sun, weak but determined, shone through a castle window and from there squeezed itself through a small hole in the wall and placed one golden finger on the little mouse" (p. 13).
   b. "Get your head out of the clouds and hunt for crumbs" (p. 18).
   c. "The song was as sweet as light shining through stained-glass windows..." (p. 29).
   d. "You have lovely ears. They are like small pieces of velvet" (p. 37).

3. Critical Thinking: The reader learns some of the ancient rules of mice. First: Do not ever, under any circumstances, reveal yourself to humans. Second: Never let a human touch you. And finally: Never speak to a human. Add to these at least two other rules you think ought to be on a list of rules a mouse should follow.

4. Poetry: A couplet is a rhymed poem of just two lines. Choose one of the characters you have met in this section and write two descriptive, rhyming lines about him or her.
   For example: Born with his eyes open wide,
   Despereaux had love inside.

Chapters 8–15, pp. 42–81

Because of his unmouselike behavior, Despereaux must face the Mouse Council. The other mice banish him to the castle dungeon, where fierce rats lurk, eager to devour Despereaux. In the deep dark of the dungeon, Despereaux tells himself to be brave like the knights in the story he read. He begins to recite the story, whereupon he meets Gregory, the castle jailer. Gregory enjoys hearing stories—a fact that saves Despereaux's life.

Vocabulary
dismay (43)
outrage (43)
indisputable (43)
renounce (44)
perfidy (45)
distinctive (51)
egregious (52)
defiance (56)
ominous (57)
burly (63)
contemplated (69)
abyss (69)
implications (71)

Discussion Questions

1. Why is it so important for Despereaux to read the words "happily ever after"? (He needs some assurance that what he is feeling and going through will, indeed, have a happy ending. pp. 46–47)

2. Do you think Despereaux really understands the reasons he was brought before the Mouse Council? Explain your answer. (Answers will vary. Students may feel that he is gradually beginning to understand what the charges are; he just does not understand why the Council does not appreciate his feelings about them. pp. 47–56)

3. On page 58 of the novel, the author asks, "Reader, do you believe that there is such a thing as happily ever after? Or, like Despereaux, have you, too, begun to question the possibility of happy endings?" When you read the author's question, what was your first reaction? Explain how you felt and why. (Answers will vary. Students should recognize that the author is creating suspense and that fantasy books generally do have a happy ending in store for the main characters.)

4. In what ways are the threadmaster's reactions to what Despereaux did different from those of the other mice? (The threadmaster seems to understand exactly what has happened to inspire Despereaux, and he is not bothered by it. The other mice are intolerant of Despereaux's lack of conformity to mouse community rules and feel threatened by his actions. pp. 59–61)

5. What is the effect of Despereaux's speaking out loud in the absolute darkness? What does it suggest about his chances of surviving in the dungeon? *(To some students it may suggest that Despereaux is not very realistic about his situation and therefore will have even more difficulty surviving. To others it may suggest a strength of character he had not previously revealed. pp. 75–81)*

6. **Prediction:** Will Gregory the jailer help Despereaux? If so, how?

Supplementary Activities

1. Storytelling: The threadmaster's words of comfort (pp. 59–61) suggest that something may have happened in his life that helps him understand how Despereaux feels. Invite students to imagine a story about the threadmaster that would explain his sympathy toward Despereaux and share the story with a classmate.

2. Literary Devices: Each of the following sentences uses a metaphor. Choose one of the metaphors and describe what picture(s) it helps you see.
   "Despereaux turned and faced the sea of mice" (p. 51).
   "…you are in the treacherous dark heart of the world" (p. 77).
   "Stories are light" (p. 81).

3. The Five Senses: Despereaux cannot see much in the dungeon, so his other senses work harder—"Despereaux listened and he was quite certain that he heard the nails and teeth of the rats, the sound of sharp things being made sharper still" (p. 78). Will your sense of hearing work harder if you cannot see? Try this experiment at home: Find a quiet spot—no television or music—and close your eyes. Listen closely for three or four minutes. Then open your eyes. Write down everything you heard. Put a check mark beside those sounds you would not usually hear. Share your results with the class the next day at school.

4. Character Analysis: Begin a Character Attribute Web (see page 9 of this guide) for Gregory the jailer.

Vocabulary
prophecy (86)
suspended (86)
illumination (88)
effective (90)
obsession (95)
domain (95)
solace (99)
tapestries (103)
minstrels (104)
spectacle (107)
revelation (109)
capacious (111)
encountered (114)
instrumental (121)

Book the Second, Chapters 16–23, pp. 85–121

Chiaroscuro—Roscuro for short—is a rat with an uncharacteristic love of light. This attraction leads him to explore the upper levels of the castle, including the banquet hall. His accidental landing in Queen Rosemary's soup is too much for her, and she dies of shock. The look of loathing Princess Pea gives the fleeing Roscuro so hurts the rat that he vows revenge. As a result of the queen's death, King Phillip outlaws soup, bowls, spoons, kettles, and rats, declaring them all illegal.

Discussion Questions

1. Why does Botticelli Remorso keep swinging the locket in front of Roscuro as he speaks to him? *(This technique is supposed to induce hypnosis. Remorso is trying to convince Roscuro to behave in a certain manner, which he can do better if he hypnotizes him. pp. 89–91)*

2. What is Botticelli's idea of a good joke? *(For the rat, a good joke is to gain a prisoner's trust by offering him whatever he wants. Then Botticelli withholds that very thing. pp. 89–90)*

3. Botticelli tells Roscuro not to go up into the light. "You will regret it," he says. (p. 96) Explain how Botticelli's prophecy comes true. *(Once Roscuro sees light, he is obsessed by it, so much so that he is determined to go upstairs in the castle. When he does so, he accidentally causes the queen's death and realizes that the lovely Princess Pea hates him. pp. 106–113)*

4. What does King Phillip hope to gain by outlawing soup in the kingdom? *(He cannot undo what has happened, but by banning soup he will not always be reminded of what happened to the queen. pp. 118–119)*

5. What is the author suggesting when she says that "every action has a consequence" (p. 118)? Do you agree with her? *(She means that every action [cause] has an effect. Answers will vary.)*

6. **Prediction:** What part will Miggery Sow play in Despereaux's life?

Supplementary Activities

1. Drama: Turn Chapter 16 into a dramatic reading and perform a skit in class. Discuss the characteristics of each character's voice. For example, Gregory's voice might be gruff but not cruel, while Botticelli's would be sinister and threatening. Conduct auditions for the narrator, Gregory, Roscuro, and Botticelli, using the appropriate voices.

2. Art: Locate the author's explanation of *chiaroscuro* (p. 85), an arrangement of light and dark. Look at Timothy Basil Ering's illustrations for this section of *The Tale of Despereaux*. Choose a scene that Ering has not illustrated and draw it using only light and dark. You may want to leave space for a caption, which should be a quote from the book.

3. Character Analysis: Complete your character web for Gregory the jailer.

4. Literary Devices: Begin a Metaphors and Similes chart (see page 10 of this guide) and list any figurative language you find as you continue to read the story. Examples: **Simile**—"He pulled the tablecloth through the bars of the cell...like a magic trick in reverse" (p. 102); **Metaphor**—mice: little packages of blood and bones (p. 96)

Vocabulary
enthusiasm (129)
scrupulously (129)
acknowledgment (131)
dour (145)
destined (151)
abundantly (151)
domestic (153)
permeated (154)
discernible (158)
detain (166)
portentous (167)
diabolical (171)

Book the Third, Chapters 24–33, pp. 125–171

Miggery Sow, a kitchen helper whose life of mistreatment has left her nearly deaf, arrives at the castle. Mig's dream is to take Pea's place as princess of the kingdom. The author relates Mig's story, describing the loss of her mother when she was six years old, her abuse at the hands of Uncle, her blunders while working at the castle, and her eventual introduction to Roscuro. Roscuro takes advantage of Mig's fantasy in order to form a plan to exact revenge on Princess Pea.

Discussion Questions

1. "Ah, child, and what does it matter what you are wanting" (p. 126)? This is what Miggery Sow's mother says to her before she dies. How do the actions of Mig's father seem to prove her statement? *(He thinks only of his own needs and wishes when he sells her into service. pp. 126–127)*

2. Based on what has happened to Mig, what do you think the author means when she says, "This is what is known as a vicious circle" (p. 130)? *(Answers will vary. Suggestion: Uncle strikes Mig on the ear if she does something wrong, which in turn makes her lose her sense of hearing. Then, because she cannot hear, she does more things wrong, starting the "circle" over again. pp. 128–130)*

3. In what way was Mig's seventh birthday a turning point in her life? *(Mig sees something beautiful—the royal entourage—and that sparks a feeling of hope inside her, something she has never had before. pp. 131–134)*

4. How would you answer the author's question on pp. 143–144 of the novel: "Reader, do you think that it is a terrible thing to hope when there is really no reason to hope at all?" *(Answers will vary.)*

5. Why is Mig able to take a tray into the dungeon without problems, unlike the serving girls who have tried it before? *(Her lack of a sense of smell and any ability to hear the dreadful things in the dungeon prevent her from feeling afraid. pp. 158–160)*

6. What might happen to Roscuro's plan of revenge, based on the clues given on page 171 of the novel? *(The "small mouselike noises of disbelief and outrage" the author describes suggest that Roscuro's plans are being overheard by Despereaux, who might try to prevent them from being carried out.)*

7. **Prediction**: Will Roscuro's plan of revenge be a success? Why or why not?

Supplementary Activities

1. Social Studies: The royal family rode out surrounded by knights in shining armor. Read about armor in a reference source and then choose one part of the armor to report on. You might, for example, choose greaves (leg armor), draw a diagram of one example, and explain where and how it was worn.

2. Art: Use different media, e.g., crayons, paints, markers, colored pencils, etc., to illustrate the brilliant light Miggery Sow saw in the distance (p. 132).

3. Perspective: Describe the scene on pages 145–150 of the novel between Miggery Sow and Princess Pea, but from the point of view of the princess. Your description should suggest what Princess Pea's thoughts and reactions might have been.

4. Writing: Create a journal such as Miggery Sow might have kept during her years with Uncle. Write two to three entries from Mig's point of view, describing her life and the things that she wishes for.

5. Literary Devices: **Simile**—"hope is like love" (p. 134); **Metaphor**—human stars: the royal family (p. 136)

Book the Fourth, Chapters 34–42, pp. 175–221

Despereaux, with Gregory the jailer's help, escapes from the dungeon, only to face Mig, armed with a kitchen knife. He gets away from her, but not before she cuts off his tail. Roscuro and Mig put their plan into motion, leading the princess deep into the dungeon. Even as she goes, Princess Pea is kindly thinking about Mig and her predicament. When Despereaux realizes that only he can save the princess' life, he goes in search of King Phillip. On his way, he happens upon a meeting of the Mouse Council. He sees his father, whom he forgives, and continues in search of the king. However, the king refuses to listen to him. Despereaux finally receives help from Hovis, the threadmaster who encouraged him when he was being taken to the dungeon.

Vocabulary

relieved (175)
miraculous (177)
skedaddle (177)
hindquarters (179)
covert (184)
comeuppance (185)
persuasion (191)
concentrated (193)
nonetheless (193)
empathetic (198)
diminishment (211)
extraordinary (221)

Discussion Questions

1. What does Mig think the outcome of Roscuro's plan will be and how does her idea of it differ from what the rat is actually planning? *(In Mig's mind, she simply switches places with the princess. Roscuro, on the other hand, intends to keep the princess in the dungeon forever. pp. 178–187)*

2. There are many symbols in this story. For example, light represents goodness, while darkness represents evil. What does soup represent? Explain your answer. *(Answers will vary. Suggestion: It symbolizes love. It was the queen's favorite food, which she shared with her husband and daughter, and Princess Pea dreams of the taste of the soup in order to find comfort when she is being taken to the dungeon. pp. 188–195)*

3. The author says, "Like most hearts, it [the princess' heart] was complicated, shaded with dark and dappled with light" (p. 197). What are the dark things in Princess Pea's heart? *(The dark things are her hatred of the rat that caused her mother's death and the sadness she feels over the loss of her mother. pp. 197–198)*

4. Given that Miggery Sow is helping the rat that the princess hates, how does Pea still manage to feel empathy for Mig? *(The princess has some knowledge of Mig's background, including her being orphaned. Being a kind person, she cannot help feeling sorry for Mig. pp. 198–199)*

5. Discuss Despereaux's realization of who he is. How has Despereaux matured since his banishment to the castle dungeon? *(When he asks the Mouse Council to admit they were wrong and they refuse, Despereaux realizes that he is different than the last time he was there. He had experienced the dungeon and survived, and he knew things they would never know. He realizes that it didn't matter what the Mouse Council or anyone else thought of him. p. 208)*

6. Describe the king's behavior after Despereaux tells him what he knows. What does this tell you about King Phillip's character? *(The king behaves very foolishly, refusing to believe anything Despereaux tells him and eventually not even listening to him at all. Answers will vary. pp. 210–215)*

7. With the threadmaster's help, Despereaux sets out to save the princess—equipped with a spool of red thread and a needle. Do you think he can succeed in his rescue attempt with only these two items? What intangibles might Despereaux be carrying with him that will help him succeed? *(Answers will vary. Suggestions for intangibles: courage, loyalty, hope, determination, and love)*

Supplementary Activities

1. Science: King Phillip says, "A mouse is but one step removed from a rat" (p. 212). Prove or disprove this statement by comparing mice and rats. Research the following characteristics for each species: size, coloring, food, home, young, and enemies. Present your conclusions in the form of a poster or chart to be displayed in the classroom.

2. Writing: Hovis the threadmaster believes that Despereaux is free because "…you're not going into the dungeon because you have to. You're going because you choose to" (p. 221). Write a brief essay explaining your interpretations of choice and freedom.

3. Art: Make an illustration of the scene in which Mig and Roscuro are leading Princess Pea down into the dungeon (pp. 196–197 of the novel).

Chapters 43–52, pp. 222–269

Having prepared himself to do what any faithful knight must do for his lady, Despereaux goes to rescue the princess from danger. However, his carefully worked-out plan fails. Instead, help comes from unexpected sources: the cook, the devious Botticelli, Miggery Sow, and even from Roscuro himself.

Vocabulary
inspiring (227)
emboldened (227)
exceptionally (237)
considerably (237)
accustomed (237)
devious (237)
cornucopia (238)
dire (240)
exaggerated (243)
infringe (249)
consigned (253)
anticipated (260)
thwarted (262)
fragile (264)
atone (267)

Discussion Questions

1. What are some of the difficulties that Despereaux has to face in order to complete his quest? *(First he has to get by the mouse-hating cook. Then, because he is such a small mouse, he has trouble with the spool of thread, which gets away from him. Next he must trust a rat to lead him to the princess. Finally, he has to defend the princess from Roscuro. pp. 226–265)*

2. How does the smell of soup affect Despereaux's courage? Why? *(The smell of it inspires him to go on. It smells delicious and probably helps him remember better times. p. 227)*

3. Give an example of how Despereaux handles his own fears when they seem about to defeat him. *(Answers will vary. Suggestion: He talks to himself, as when he stands at the top of the dungeon stairs and peers into the darkness. pp. 236–237)*

4. What are Botticelli's real motives for leading Despereaux to the princess? *(He wants to see the mouse suffer by leading him to what he loves most and then denying it to him. p. 244)*

5. What causes Mig to shift her plans—from becoming a princess to saving one? *(Once Princess Pea is in the dungeon, Roscuro reveals his real plan. Mig realizes that Roscuro never intended to help her become a princess, and he treats her just like everyone else has always treated her. Roscuro calls her a fool and tells her that no one cares what she wants. Mig has had enough, and she determines to save herself and the princess from the rat. pp. 252–253)*

6. What promise changes Roscuro's plans? *(The princess promises that if he saves them, she will let him eat soup in the banquet hall. pp. 264–265)*

7. How is Princess Pea able to show kindness to Roscuro after all he's done? *(The princess knows how fragile her heart is and how the dark parts struggle with the light parts. She forgives Roscuro and promises him happiness in order to save her own heart. p. 264)*

Supplementary Activities

1. Social Studies: Gather soup recipes from family members and others. Combine your recipes with those of your classmates and copy five or six of your favorite ones to create a gift book. Then decorate the pages with art and quotes from *The Tale of Despereaux* about the desirability of eating soup.

2. Art: Have your teacher assist you in creating puppets for the characters in this section and use them to act out the final dramatic scene in the dungeon. To make the body parts movable (and the tails removable), you can use paper fasteners. Additional materials you will need are tag board, scissors, paints or felt-tip markers, string, and cardboard.

3. Poetry: Read the author's statement on page 258 of the novel: "Reader, nothing is sweeter in this sad world than the sound of someone you love calling your name." Do you agree or disagree? Write a poem reflecting your opinion.

Post-reading Discussion Questions

1. On the invitation page (p. 7), the author says, "The world is dark, and light is precious." Then, on page 270, the author's coda, or final word, reads, "Stories are light...Reader, I hope you have found some light here." Do you feel that the author has achieved her goal of bringing you light? Why do you think so?

2. The author explains that the character of Despereaux came from her wish to write about "an unlikely hero." Based on what you read in this novel and in other books, what would a likely hero be?

3. Suppose you could meet Kate DiCamillo and ask her to write a particular kind of book. What would you ask for?

4. Look at the title page and read the full title of the novel: *The Tale of Despereaux being the story of a mouse, a princess, some soup, and a spool of thread.* Do you think this full title is a good summary of the book? What would you add to it or replace it with?

5. Who was your favorite character in the novel and why?

6. Who was the least likable character in the novel? What did you learn about that character that made him or her so unlikable?

7. What did you learn from this novel about love? courage? hope?

8. What do you think is the most important event in the story? What other events happen as a result of it?

9. Do any of the characters, human or animal, remind you of people you know? In what way?

10. Would you recommend this book to a friend? Why or why not?

Post-reading Extension Activities

1. Write a riddle that describes a character in the novel. Include clues that will help other students picture this character. Describe how this character looks, feels, talks, and how other characters in the story treat him or her.

2. The characters in this novel do some things right and other things wrong. Choose one character and write him or her a letter about things to be prepared for in the future so that he or she will not make the same mistakes again.

3. Based on what you learned from the author's story of "an unlikely hero," write yourself a reminder about judging someone solely by his or her appearance.

4. Despereaux loves stories about knights and quests. Find a book that he would like. Choose one part you think he would like and read it aloud to a classmate.

5. Imagine doing a television interview with one of the characters in the final scene of the novel (pp. 266–269). Invite a classmate to act out the interview with you.

6. Write a letter from Despereaux to his family describing his adventures in the castle.

7. Make a collage that represents many different symbols of light and dark, e.g., white/black, the sun/the moon, a mountaintop/a cave. Use your own illustrations or pictures cut out of newspapers or magazines.

8. If you enjoyed Kate DiCamillo's writing, ask a librarian for other books by her or by other authors who write about similar subjects. Check off the books you plan to read and invite your classmates to do the same.

9. Complete the Effects of Reading chart on page 11 of this guide.

Assessment for *The Tale of Despereaux*

Assessment is an ongoing process. The following nine items can be completed during the novel study. Once finished, the student and teacher will check the work. Points may be added to indicate the level of understanding.

Name _____ Date _____

Student   **Teacher**

_____   _____   1. Working in a small group, write five review questions for your assigned section. Participate in an oral review.

_____   _____   2. Complete the Story Map on page 12 of this guide.

_____   _____   3. Write a short summary of the book, using at least ten vocabulary words.

_____   _____   4. As the teacher calls out certain character traits, write the name of the character in the book you think best matches each trait.

_____   _____   5. Write a two-line description of one of the characters, but omit the name. Exchange descriptions with a partner and identify the character s/he has described.

_____   _____   6. Set up an acrostic. Write the letters of one of the qualities Despereaux reveals (determination, loyalty, bravery, idealism, forgiveness) vertically on a piece of lined paper. Then write a series of sentences, each of which begins with one of the letters in the word and tells something about how the character developed the quality.

_____   _____   7. Correct all mistakes on quizzes.

_____   _____   8. Display or perform your extension activity on the assigned day.

_____   _____   9. Working with a small group, prepare a skit for one of the major scenes from the book. Perform it for the class and have your classmates guess which scene your group is performing.

Reading Comprehension Assessment

Directions: Answer the questions below in the space provided. Support your answers with examples from the novel.

1. Describe one conflict that Despereaux faces and explain how it makes him stronger.

   _____

   _____

   _____

   _____

   _____

2. Explain what the "light" and "darkness" symbolize in *The Tale of Despereaux*.

   _____

   _____

   _____

   _____

   _____

Linking Novel Units® Activities to National and State Reading Assessments

During the past several years, an increasing number of students have faced some form of state-mandated competency testing in reading. Many states now administer reading assessments to measure the skills and knowledge emphasized in their particular reading curriculum. This Novel Units® Teacher Guide includes optional comprehension questions that correlate with state-mandated reading assessments. The rubric below provides important information for evaluating responses to open-ended comprehension questions. Teachers may also use scoring rubrics provided for their own state's competency test.

Scoring Rubric for Open-Ended Items

3-Exemplary	Thorough, complete ideas/information Clear organization throughout Logical reasoning/conclusions Thorough understanding of reading task Accurate, complete response
2-Sufficient	Many relevant ideas/pieces of information Clear organization throughout most of response Minor problems in logical reasoning/conclusions General understanding of reading task Generally accurate and complete response
1-Partially Sufficient	Minimally relevant ideas/information Obvious gaps in organization Obvious problems in logical reasoning/conclusions Minimal understanding of reading task Inaccuracies/incomplete response
0-Insufficient	Irrelevant ideas/information No coherent organization Major problems in logical reasoning/conclusions Little or no understanding of reading task Generally inaccurate/incomplete response

Glossary

Book the First, Chapters 1–7, pp. 11–41
disappointment (12): something or someone that fails to satisfy
tragedy (12): an event involving injury or loss of life
intent (18): firmly fixed or concentrated on a purpose
siblings (20): brothers and/or sisters
molding (21): a strip of wood used to decorate a surface
indignant (24): filled with anger
circumstances (27): conditions
incredible (30): astonishing
adoringly (32): regarding with extreme love and affection
protested (38): objected; disagreed
ancient (39): very old

Chapters 8–15, pp. 42–81
dismay (43): a sudden loss of courage
outrage (43): resentful anger
indisputable (43): undeniable; beyond doubt
renounce (44): to give up by formal announcement
perfidy (45): deliberate violation of faith or trust
distinctive (51): characteristic; typical
egregious (52): bad; offensive
defiance (56): bold resistance to authority
ominous (57): menacing; threatening
burly (63): heavy, strong, and muscular
contemplated (69): looked at carefully and thoughtfully
abyss (69): a profound depth; a void
implications (71): meanings; consequences

Book the Second, Chapters 16–23, pp. 85–121
prophecy (86): a prediction of the future
suspended (86): to hang so as to allow free movement
illumination (88): a source of light
effective (90): to produce a strong response
obsession (95): a compulsive preoccupation with an idea or emotion
domain (95): a territory of activity or function
solace (99): comfort; consolation
tapestries (103): heavy, colorful cloths hung for decoration
minstrels (104): musicians or poets
spectacle (107): something of a remarkable or impressive nature
revelation (109): a dramatic disclosure of an unknown fact
capacious (111): large; spacious
encountered (114): to come upon
instrumental (121): helpful; implemental

Book the Third, Chapters 24–33, pp. 125–171

enthusiasm (129): great excitement or interest
scrupulously (129): exactly; painstakingly
acknowledgment (131): recognition; formal declaration
dour (145): stern; unyielding
destined (151): assigned for a specific purpose or end
abundantly (151): greatly; plentiful
domestic (153): relating to the family or the household
permeated (154): spread; flowed throughout
discernible (158): perceptible
detain (166): delay; keep
portentous (167): exciting; wonderful; awesome
diabolical (171): wicked; cruel

Book the Fourth, Chapters 34–42, pp. 175–221

relieved (175): freed from pain, anxiety, or stress
miraculous (177): astounding; unbelievable
skedaddle (177): to leave quickly
hindquarters (179): the posterior part of an animal
covert (184): secretive
comeuppance (185): a deserved punishment or retribution
persuasion (191): the act of convincing someone to believe, act, or feel a certain way
concentrated (193): focused
nonetheless (193): however
empathetic (198): able to understand another's situation, feelings, or motives
diminishment (211): reduction; lessening
extraordinary (221): remarkable; unusual

Chapters 43–52, pp. 222–269

inspiring (227): able to affect deeply
emboldened (227): to be encouraged
exceptionally (237): uncommonly; abnormally
considerably (237): greatly; immensely
accustomed (237): adapted or used to
devious (237): shifty; sly
cornucopia (238): an abundance; a great amount
dire (240): fearsome; urgent; desperate
exaggerated (243): represented as larger or greater than it actually is
infringe (249): to trespass or violate
consigned (253): entrusted; turned over to the care of
anticipated (260): expected
thwarted (262): prevented; defeated
fragile (264): easily broken, damaged, or destroyed
atone (267): to make amends; repent

Notes

© Novel Units, Inc.